JUN 0 5 2014

D0646297

The Good-Pie Party

written by Liz Garton Scanlon

illustrated by Kady MacDonald Denton

Arthur A. Levine Books • An Imprint of Scholastic Inc.

Text copyright © 2014 by Liz Garton Scanlon
Illustrations copyright © 2014 by Kady MacDonald Denton

All rights reserved. Published by Arthur A. Levine Books, an imprint of Scholastic Inc., *Publishers since 1920.*
SCHOLASTIC and the LANTERN LOGO are trademarks and/or registered trademarks of Scholastic Inc.

No part of this publication may be reproduced, stored in a retrieval system, or transmitted in any form or by any means, electronic, mechanical, photocopying, recording, or otherwise, without written permission of the publisher. For information regarding permission, write to Scholastic Inc., Attention: Permissions Department, 557 Broadway, New York, NY 10012.

Library of Congress Cataloging-in-Publication Data
Scanlon, Elizabeth Garton.
The Good-Pie Party / by Liz Garton Scanlon ; illustrated by Kady MacDonald Denton. – First edition.   pages cm
Summary: Posy Peyton and her friends are very sad that she will be moving away, but when they try
to cheer themselves up by baking a pie, they realize that Posy's leaving does not have to mean saying good-bye.
ISBN 978-0-545-44870-3 (hardcover : alk. paper) [1. Moving, Household – Fiction. 2. Friendship – Fiction.
3. Baking – Fiction. 4. Pies – Fiction. 5. Parties – Fiction.] I. Denton, Kady MacDonald, illustrator. II. Title.
PZ7.S2798Goo 2014   [E] – dc23   2013006975

10 9 8 7 6 5 4 3 2 1   14 15 16 17 18

Printed in China   38
First edition, April 2014

The artwork was created using pen and ink and watercolor on hot-pressed watercolor paper.
Display type was set in Swingdancer. The text type was set in Caslon Book BE.
Book design by Chelsea C. Donaldson

For Erin Murphy,
Agent à la Mode — L. G. S.

To Jill — K. M. D.

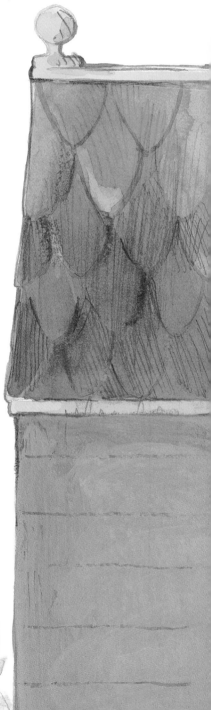

Posy Peyton doesn't want to move.

She doesn't want to pack her books
or take down her bird feeder
or undecorate her secret clubhouse.

And she really doesn't want to say good-bye.

"My mom says we should enjoy the time we have," says Megan,
getting into position for the perfect pyramid.

"You can't even make a
pyramid without three
people," says Posy,
climbing glumly to the top.

"*My* mom says we should count our lucky stars we're such good friends," says Mae, unpinning pictures from the wall.

"We might as well call them *un*lucky stars now," says Posy, pulling the curtains closed.

"*My* mom says we should have a good-bye party."
Posy shuts the door behind them.

"But then we'd have to say good-bye!" say Megan and Mae.

"I know," says Posy. "That's what I mean."

Back inside the house, every room is boxed up but the kitchen.

"There's nothing to do but bake," sighs Posy.

"Pie?" asks Megan.

"We'll help," says Mae.

So the girls roll out dough and push it into a deep glass pan.
They peel apples and sprinkle them with cinnamon and cloves.
They crimp the edges of the pale white crust.

"It smells delicious in here!" says Posy's mom.

"Humph," answers Posy, even though she's feeling a little bit better already.

"We're making pie," says Megan.

"Hot, sweet, good pie," says Mae.

"Wait!" says Posy. "Good *pie*! Good pie is *better* than good-bye!"

Mom laughs. So do Megan and Mae.

"What about a good-*pie* party, Mom?" asks Posy. "I *like* that idea!"

As it turns out, *everyone* does.

So the girls make plans and invitations, one by one.

"Don't forget the Youngs," says Posy's dad
from behind a stack of newspapers.

"Or Ms. McMalley," calls Mom from the coat closet.

"Or Roman," says Posy.

"Or Lucy," says Megan.

"Or Jane," says Mae.

The list grows and grows, and the next afternoon
everyone arrives with lawn chairs and cameras . . .

. . . and pie upon pie upon pie.

Posy spoons out whipping cream.

Megan and Mae pour lemonade.

All the kids make a huge pyramid.

As the sun sinks, Posy's dad asks
if she'd like to make a toast.

"To good friends," Posy calls.

"Good friends!" answers everyone.

"And good-pie," she says, with a little lump in her throat.

"Good-pie," whisper Megan and Mae, with lumps in theirs.

When everyone leaves, the girls stretch out on the grass
and stare at the lopsided moon.

"Look," says Posy, "even the sky brought a pie."

"That's one we can always share," says Megan.

"Even when you move away," says Mae.

"Lucky us," says Posy as the stars start to shine.

"Lucky us," say Megan and Mae.